For my darling friend Tanya and
her little angel Sofia Isabelle Parton

First published 2021 by Two Hoots
an imprint of Pan Macmillan
The Smithson, 6 Briset Street
London EC1M 5NR
EU representative: Macmillan Publishers Ireland Limited,
Mallard Lodge, Lansdowne Village, Dublin 4

Associated companies throughout the world
www.panmacmillan.com
ISBN 978-1-5290-5051-6

1 3 5 7 9 8 6 4 2
A CIP catalogue record for this book is available from the British Library.
Printed in China
The illustrations in this book were created using
pen, ink, gouache and Photoshop.

www.twohootsbooks.com

THE TRUTH ABOUT BABIES

Elina Ellis

TWO HOOTS

It is nearly time for the baby to be born.

"You'll love the new baby!"

"Babies are the best."

"You must be excited."

"Babies are so much fun!"

My family seems to know
a lot about babies.

They say babies are.

BEAUTIFUL.

. . . and babies

REALLY

LOVE

SLEEPING.

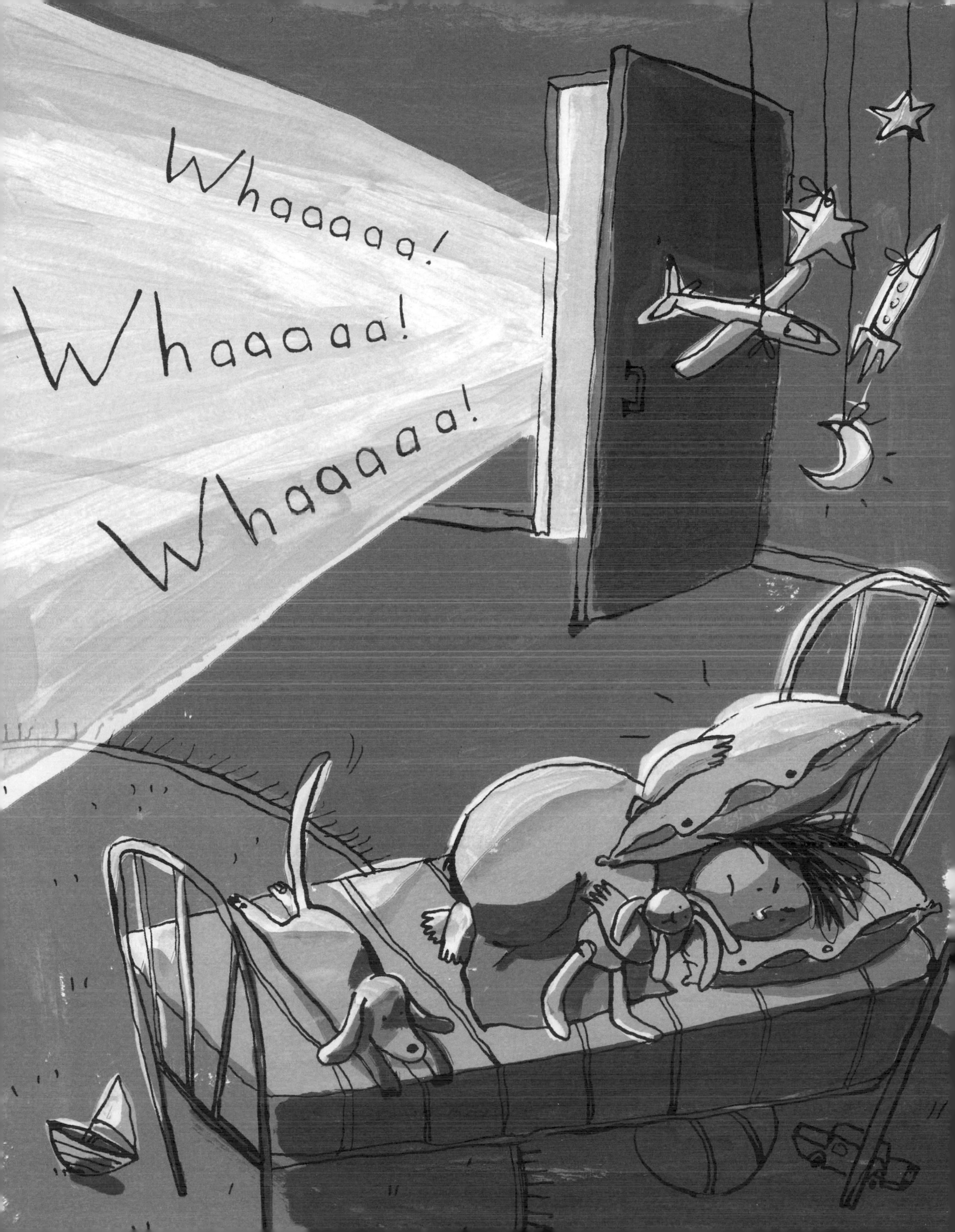

Whaaaaa!

Whaaaaaa!

Whaaaaaa!

They say babies are . . .

CUTE

LITTLE

BUNDLES

OF JOY.

Apparently babies

SMELL

LOVELY.

Ow!
They tell me babies
are SWEET,
DELICATE...
Oy!

and SO VERY GENTLE.

They say babies are
PERFECT ANGELS.

But I know the

TRUTH

about babies.

THEY ARE LITTLE

MONSTERS!

But I still love
my brother.

He is the sweetest, cutest, loveliest baby

EVER!

And he's my favourite little monster.